PUFFIN BOOKS

THE LITTLE WITCH
AND 5 OTHER FAVOURITES

Poor but kind-hearted sailor Jack decides to adopt twenty orphans, but the only way he can get enough money is to become a dashing pirate! He's not really cut out to be part of the wildest band of pirates that ever flew the Jolly Roger, and soon the captain sees that Jack's heart isn't in his work. 'Jack, you son-of-a-sea-cook . . . why don't you spend your money in wild and riotous living like a pirate should, instead of hoarding it, like a magpie or a landlubber, in that suitcase under your bunk?' The only thing they can do with him, according to pirate rules, is to maroon him, and so poor Jack is left on the strangest island in the world where the oddest things happen!

Sailor Jack is just one of the strange but lovable characters in these six funny and fantastic tales, all of which were first published as picture books.

Margaret Mahy is a New Zealander who has been writing stories since the age of seven. She writes for a wide age range and has been awarded the Carnegie Medal twice and the Esther Glen Award three times. She lives near Christchurch, South Island, and has two grown-up daughters, several cats, a large garden and thousands of books. Her books for Puffin include *Raging Robots and Unruly Uncles*, *The Downhill Crocodile Whizz* and *A Lion in the Meadow* (Picture Puffin).

Margaret Mahy

The Little Witch
and
5
other Favourites

Illustrated by Jenny Williams

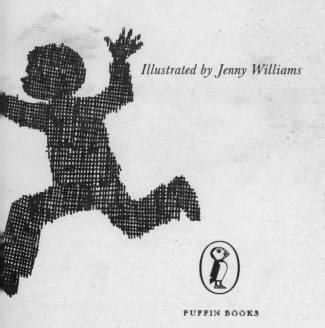

PUFFIN BOOKS

Puffin Books, Penguin Books Ltd, Harmondsworth, Middlesex, England
Viking Penguin Inc., 40 West 23rd Street, New York, New York 10010, U.S.A.
Penguin Books Australia Ltd, Ringwood, Victoria, Australia
Penguin Books Limited, 2801 John Street, Markham, Ontario, Canada L3R 1B4
Penguin Books (N.Z.) Ltd, 182–190 Wairau Road, Auckland 10, New Zealand

This collection (with different illustrations)
first published under the title *A Lion in the Meadow and 5 Other Favourites*
by J. M. Dent & Sons Ltd, 1976
Published in Puffin Books 1987

These stories were originally published in the New Zealand *School Journal*,
New Zealand Department of Education

Made and printed in Great Britain by
Cox & Wyman Ltd, Reading, Berks

Typeset in 14/18 Baskerville
by Rowland Phototypesetting Ltd
Bury St Edmunds, Suffolk

Contents

A Lion in the Meadow

The little boy said,
  'Mother, there is a lion in the meadow.'
  The mother said,
  'Nonsense, little boy.'
  The little boy said,
  'Mother, there is a big yellow lion in the meadow.'
  The mother said,

'Nonsense, little boy.'

The little boy said,

'Mother, there is a big, roaring, yellow, whiskery lion in the meadow!'

The mother said,

'Little boy, you are making up stories again. There is nothing in the meadow but grass and trees. Go into the meadow and see for yourself.'

The little boy said,

'Mother, I'm scared to go into the meadow because of the lion which is there.'

The mother said,

'Little boy, you are making up stories – so I will make up a story, too . . . Do you see this match box? Take it out into the meadow and open it. In it will be a tiny dragon. The tiny dragon will grow into a big dragon. It will chase the lion away.'

The little boy took the match box and went away. The mother went on peeling the potatoes.

Suddenly the door opened.

In rushed a big, roaring, yellow, whiskery lion.

'Hide me!' it said. 'A dragon is after me!'

The lion hid in the broom cupboard.

Then the little boy came running in.

'Mother,' he said. 'That dragon grew too big. There is no lion in the meadow now. There is a DRAGON in the meadow.'

The little boy hid in the broom cupboard too.

'You should have left me alone,' said the lion. 'I eat only apples.'

'But there wasn't a real dragon,' said the mother. 'It was just a story I made up.'

'It turned out to be true after all,' said the little boy. 'You should have looked in the match box first.'

'That is how it is,' said the lion. 'Some stories are true, and some aren't . . .

'But I have an idea. We will go and play in the meadow on the other side of the house. There is no dragon there.'

'I am glad we are friends now,' said the little boy.

The little boy and the big roaring yellow whiskery lion went to play in the other meadow.

The dragon stayed where he was, and nobody minded.

The mother never ever made up a story again.

Sailor Jack and the 20 Orphans

There was once a boy called Tom who was an orphan and who lived with nineteen other orphans in a big house called Bartholomew's Institution. They had no father, only a Board of Governors.

And there was once a sailor called Jack, who had sailed all round the seven seas seven times. Tom and Jack met on a wharf where they liked to sit, dangling their legs over the edge. Tom loved listening to stories and Jack loved telling them, so they got on very well.

The story Tom liked best was when Jack told how he had fought the terrible giant oyster, and how he had been captured by the Monkey King. Tom listened as if he had ten ears to keep busy, instead of only two.

All the time Jack was talking the tide came up and up, trying to get at their dangling feet, and they did not even notice it.

Then Tom explained that he was one of twenty boy orphans who loved sea stories, and he told Jack all about Bartholomew's Institution. Jack listened amazed.

'It sounds a poor life to me,' he said at last. 'I'll tell you what! I've always had a fancy to adopt some boys to be my sons and listen to my stories. Now it seems to me that twenty is a good satisfying number. I'll save up my money,

and, this time next year, I'll come back and adopt you all. How's *that* for an idea?'

'It's a splendid idea!' Tom cried. 'The best you ever had! I will meet you here in a year's time (I'll bring the other orphans too). Then you can adopt us, and we'll all go to sea together.'

Hardly had they settled this, when the tide slopped into their shoes, so that they knew it was time to say goodbye. They shook hands and each went his way, after promising once more to meet there in a year's time.

Well, how does a poor sailor like Jack get enough money to adopt twenty orphans? He becomes a dashing pirate! This is what Jack did. He joined one of the wildest crews that ever flew the Jolly Roger.

Unfortunately, though he got on well with his saving of money, he got on badly with the pirates. They were a slouching grubby lot, and, though they were brave and bold at fighting with swords, the thought of soap and water made them turn as pale as cheese. (Jack, of course, was smart and polite and washed at least once a day.)

Then too, the pirates spent all their money in a wasteful and reckless fashion, whereas Jack saved all his, hoping to get enough to adopt his twenty orphans.

One day the pirate Captain up and said to Jack:

'Jack, you son-of-a-sea-cook, it seems to me your heart isn't in your work. Why don't you spend your money in wild and riotous living like a pirate should, instead of hoarding it, like a magpie or a landlubber, in that suitcase under your bunk?'

'Well, I'm saving it for this and that,' said Jack. 'Notably because I have it in mind to adopt twenty orphan boys to be my sons.'

The pirate Captain's mouth fell open, and he was so put about with surprise that he could not speak.

'Jack!' he cried at last. 'You'll never make a

pirate! Orphans, indeed! Where's your knavery and wickedness!

'Jack,' he roared, 'we'll have to maroon you! No one is more sorry than myself, but there you are – it's one of the pirate rules.'

'I'm always willing to keep the rules, Captain,' said Jack smartly, 'no matter how much discomfort it may mean to me personally.'

Marooning means that a sailor is left alone on an island with nothing but his clothes, some salt pork, and a box of matches. On the first island they came to the pirates marooned Jack, taking his share of the treasure away with them. He was left alone on the strangest little island in the world.

It was strange because it was a long and pointed little island and because it had one tall

palm tree on it. And it was strange because, although it had only one palm tree, it had fifty monkeys who leaped and chattered at Jack and followed him everywhere he went.

Lastly it was strange because on the top of the palm tree perched an old poll parrot with a telescope under its wing, which isn't a thing you'd find on most islands.

'Well,' said Jack, 'I've sailed the seven seas seven times, but never have I seen such an island.'

Night fell, and it was cold – so cold that Jack felt his bones were turning to ice. How does a freezing sailor warm himself up? He dances hornpipes up and down the beach and sings a sea shanty. This is what Jack did. Faster and faster he danced and, as he did so, he thought he felt the island rock beneath him though he was as light of foot and as nimble as a sea cook's cat.

'Now that's odd,' Jack thought, 'islands shouldn't rock as easily as that.'

As he thought this thought, he was surprised to hear a deep voice call:

'Who is that whose heel and toe
Make my island rocking go?'

Jack answered quickly and grammatically:

'It is I, good sailor John,
Trying to keep my trotters warm.'

Then suddenly, at his very feet, a cave opened in the silver sand and out came a tall woman dressed in a dress of seaweed and shell, with ropes of pearls around her neck and a wonderful magical cap made of crayfish shell. All Jack could do was to stare in admiration and say . . .

'What a fine figure of a woman my eyes do now behold!'

'You may well say so,' she replied. 'My name is Jones, Miss Emily Jones, one of the famous submarine family of Davy Jones, who has a well-known locker. And who are you, Sailor Jack, and what are you doing on my island?'

'Ma'am,' said Jack, 'I was marooned here by pirates, something for which I'm very sorry. But having met you, why it becomes a pleasure and a privilege to be marooned on your floating island.'

'Nicely put!' said Emily Jones, bowing like a sea wave, 'but why did they maroon you?'

So Jack told her the whole story, while the moon rose higher and the monkeys crept round to listen too.

At the end of the tale Emily Jones sighed and said sadly, 'Indeed Jack, I feel for you something tremendous. I have often thought I'd like twenty boys myself.'

Then Jack looked at the moon and thought he saw it wink at him, so speaking out boldly, as you'd expect such a sailor to speak, he said, 'Madam, let's adopt the twenty boys together, for since I began to tell you the tale, it has occurred to me that, as well as twenty sons, I'd like a wife. And it has also occurred to me that you are the lass I'd like to marry – if you would be willing to accept the hand of a simple sailor.'

Emily Jones blushed in the moonlight and looked at her feet in their oyster shell shoes.

'Why Jack,' she said, 'to be brisk and sea-manlike, as becomes a member of the Jones family, the answer's "Yes!" for I never met a man, fresh or salt, that I liked better.'

'Well now,' said Jack, 'you've made me the happiest man on the seven seas! Now let's think of how to get to the wharf and meet Tom and the other orphans so that we can adopt them, for there *they* are, and here *we* are, and we've got to get from here to there.'

'As to that,' said Emily, 'it's as easy as sneezing, for this island is *more* than an island. It is a boat, too! I am the captain, the monkeys are the crew, and the parrot is a lookout. Moreover, Jack, you don't need to worry about money for I have a fortune in pearls from my pet oysters.' And she led him to a vine-covered shed full of gleaming pearls of all sizes.

Then said Jack, '*You* are the brightest treasure of the island, my pretty cat-fish, but we shall have a use for those pearls. Get your clever and amusing monkeys to hoist the sail and ho for the wharf and our twenty orphans.'

So that is what they did. They came home to the wharf just exactly a year after Sailor Jack had left it. There was Tom, waiting for Jack, and with him were his orphan friends (the whole nineteen of them) and the Board of Governors from Bartholomew's Institution. As Jack and Emily sailed up the harbour, all the big boats and all the little ones blew their whistles and sirens, while all the sailors danced hornpipes and sang sea shanties, for they knew it was no ordinary sailor who came into port on a floating island with monkeys for a crew.

'I knew you'd come,' said Tom.

'Well, I won't say it wasn't a struggle to get here,' said Jack, 'but here I am.'

Luckily one of the Board of Governors was a Minister of the Church, so Jack and Emily got married straight away.

Then Sailor Jack and his bride gave the Board of Governors two barrels of pearls (one of white pearls and the other of pink), and they quickly adopted the twenty orphans. So now there was a family of twenty boys, a mother (Emily) and a father (Jack), all of them going to live on board the little floating island.

Of course the Board of Governors invited them to stay for dinner.

'Thank you kindly,' Jack answered, 'but me and my new wife Emily must get out on our honeymoon with our twenty boys. We're going to have adventures such as you have never dreamed of. Aren't we, Emily? Aren't we, Tom?'

'We are!' said Emily and Tom firmly.

And 'We are!' shouted all the nineteen boys.

'Some might say this is the happy ending,' said Jack, 'but I say, brisk and seaman-like as is my nature, it is just the happy beginning.'

Then the parrot shouted, 'Hoist aloft the sails!' The monkeys began to climb the palm tree, and the island moved merrily out of the harbour into the sunset. The Board of Governors waved goodbye.

'Perhaps they will come back,' they said.

But the floating island, Jack, Emily, and the boys never ever came back again, for they were bound for places of enchantment about which no ordinary tale dares to tell.

The Little Witch

The big city was dark. Even the streetlights were out. All day people had gone up and down, up and down; cars and trams and trams and buses had roared and rattled busily along. But now they had all gone home to bed, and only the wind, the shadows, and a small kitten wandered in the wide, still streets.

The kitten chased a piece of paper, pretending it was a mouse. He patted at it with his paws and it flipped behind a rubbish bin. Quick as a wink he leaped after it, and then forgot it because he had found something else.

'What is this,' he asked the wind, 'here asleep behind the rubbish bin? I have never seen it before.'

The wind was bowling a newspaper along, but he dropped it and came to see. The great

stalking shadows looked down from everywhere.

'Ah,' said the wind, 'it is a witch . . . see her
broomstick . . . but she is only a very small one.'

The wind was right. It was a very small witch
– a baby one.

The little witch heard the wind in her sleep
and opened her eyes. Suddenly she was awake.

Far above, the birds peered down at the
street below.

'Look!' said the shadows to the sparrows

26

under the eaves. 'Look at the little witch; she is such a little witch to be all alone.'

'Let me see!' a baby sparrow peeped sleepily.

'Go to sleep!' said his mother. 'I didn't hatch you out of the egg to peer at witches all night long.'

She snuggled him back into her warm feathers.

But there was no one to snuggle a little witch, wandering cold in the big empty streets, dragging a broom several sizes too big for her. The kitten sprang at the broom. Then he noticed something.

'Wind!' he cried. 'See! – wherever this witch walks, she leaves a trail of flowers!'

Yes, it is true! The little witch had lots of magic in her, but she had not learned to use it properly, or to hide it, any more than she had learned to talk.

So wherever she put her feet mignonette grew, and rosemary, violets, lily of the valley, and tiny pink-and-white roses . . . all through the streets, all across the road . . .

Butterflies came, from far and wide, to dance and drink.

'Who is that down there?' asked a young moth.

'It is a baby witch who has made these fine, crimson feast-rooms for us,' a tattered old moth answered.

The wind followed along, playing and juggling with the flowers and their sweet smells. 'I shall sweep these all over the city,' he said. In their sleep, people smelled the flowers and smiled, dreaming happily.

Now the witch looked up at the tall buildings; windows looked down at her with scorn, and their square sharp shapes seemed angry to her. She pointed her finger at them.

Out of the cracks and chinks suddenly crept long twining vines and green leaves. Slowly flowers opened on them . . . great crimson flowers like roses, smelling of honey.

The little witch laughed, but in a moment she became solemn. She was so alone. Then the kitten scuttled and pounced at her bare, pink heels, and the little witch knew she had a friend. Dragging her broom for the kitten to chase, she wandered on, leaving a trail of flowers.

Now the little witch stood in the street, very small and lost, and cold in her blue smock and bare feet.

She pointed up at the city clock tower, and it became a huge fir tree, while the clock face turned into a white nodding owl and flew away!

The owl flew as fast as the wind to a tall dark castle perched high on a hill. There at the window sat a slim, tired witch-woman, looking out into the night. 'Where, oh where is my little baby witch? I must go and search for her again.'

'Whoo! Whoo!' cried the owl. 'There is a little witch down in the city and she is enchanting everything. What will the people say tomorrow?'

The witch-woman rode her broomstick through the sky and over the city, looking eagerly down through the mists. Far below she could see the little witch running and hiding in doorways, while the kitten chased after her.

Down flew the witch-woman – down, down
to a shop doorway. The little witch and the
kitten stopped and stared at her.

'Why,' said the witch-woman, in her dark

velvety voice, 'you are my own dear little witch
. . . my lost little witch!' She held out her arms
and the little witch ran into them. She wasn't
lost any more.

The witch-woman looked around at the en-
chanted city, and she smiled. 'I'll leave it as it
is,' she said, 'for a surprise tomorrow.'

Then she gathered the little witch onto her
broomstick, and the kitten jumped on, too, and
off they went to their tall castle home, with

windows as deep as night, and lived there happily ever after.

And the next day when the people got up and came out to work, the city was full of flowers and the echoes of laughter.

The Man Whose
Mother was a Pirate

There was once a little man who had never seen
the sea, although his mother was an old pirate
woman. The two of them lived in a great city,
far, far from the seashore.

The little man had a brown suit with black buttons, and a brown tie and shiny shoes – all most respectable and handsome. He worked in a neat office and wrote down rows of figures in books, and ruled lines under them. And before he spoke, he always coughed '*Hrrrrrm!*'

Well, one day his mother said, 'Shipmate, I want to see the sea again. I want to get the city smoke out of my lungs and put the sea salt there instead. I want to fire my old silver pistol off again, and see the waves jump with surprise.'

'*Hrrrrm*, Mother,' the little man said, very respectful and polite. 'I haven't got a car or even a horse, and no money to get one or the other. All we have is a wheelbarrow and a kite.'

'We must make do,' his mother answered sharply. 'I will go and load my silver pistol and polish my cutlass.'

The little man went to work. He asked Mr Fat (who was the man he worked for), '*Hrrrrm*, Mr Fat! May I have two weeks to take my mother to the seaside?'

'I don't go to the seaside,' Mr Fat snapped out. 'Why should you need to go?'

'*Hrrrrm*, it is for my mother,' the little man explained.

'I don't see why you should want to go to the seaside,' said Mr Fat, crossly. 'There is nothing there but water . . . salty at that! I once found a penny in the sand, but that is all the money I have ever made at the seaside. There is nothing financial about the sea.'

'*Hrrrrm*, it is for my mother,' the little man said again. 'I will be back in two weeks.'

'Make sure you are!' Mr Fat answered crossly.

So they set off, the little man pushing his mother in the wheelbarrow, and his mother holding the kite.

His mother's short grey hair ruffled merrily out under the green scarf she wore tied around her head. Her gold earrings challenged the sun, throwing his own light back to him.

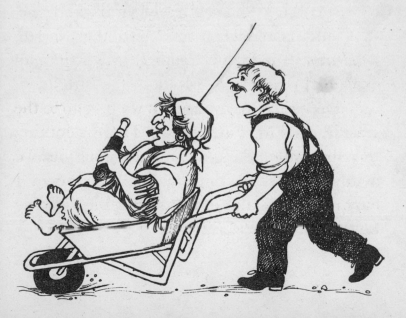

Between her lips was her old black pipe, and she wore, behind her ear, a rose that matched her scarlet shawl. The little man wore his brown suit and boots, all buttoned and tied. He trotted along pushing the wheelbarrow.

As they went, his mother talked about the sea. She told him of its voices:

'It sings at night with a sad booming voice. Under the sun it laughs and slaps the side of the ship in time to its laughter. Yes, and then, when a storm comes, it screams and hates poor sailors. And the sea is a great gossip! What is the weather at Tierra del Fuego? Is the ice moving in Hudson Bay? Where are the great whales sailing? The sea knows it all, and one wave mutters and whispers it to another, and to those who know how to listen.'

'*Hrrrrm*, yes indeed, Mother,' the little man said, pattering the wheelbarrow along. His shoes hurt rather.

'Where are you going?' a farming fellow asked him.

'*Hrrrrm*, I'm taking Mother to the seaside,' the little man answered.

'I wouldn't go there,' the farming fellow remarked. 'It's not a safe place at all. It's wet and cold and gritty, I'm told . . . not comfortable like a cowshed.'

'*Hrrrrm*, it's very musical, Mother says,' the little man replied.

In his mind he heard the laughter and the boom and the scream and the song of the sea. He trotted along, pushing the wheelbarrow. His mother rested her chin on her knees as she jolted along.

39

'Yes, it is blue in the sunshine,' she said. 'And when the sun goes in, the sea becomes green. Yet in the twilight I have seen it grey and serene, and at night, inky-black and wild, it tosses beside the ship. Sunrise turns it to burning gold, the moon to liquid silver. There is always change in the sea.'

They came to a river . . . There was no boat.

The little man tied the wheelbarrow, with his mother in it, to the kite string. His neat little moustache was wild and ruffled by the wind. Now he ran barefoot.

'*Hrrrrm!* Hold on tight, Mother,' he called.

Up in the air they went as the wind took the kite with it. The little man dangled from the kite string and his mother swung in her wheelbarrow basket.

'This is all very well, Sam,' she shouted to him, 'but the sea – ah the sea! It rocks you to sleep, tosses you in the air, pulls you down to the deep. It speeds you along and holds you still. It storms you and calms you. The sea is bewitching but bewildering.'

'*Hrrrrm*, yes, Mother,' the little man said. As

he dangled from the kite string he saw the sea in his mind – the blue and the green of it, the rise and the fall, the white wings of the birds, the white wings of the ships.

The kite let them down gently on the other side of the river.

'Where are you going?' asked a philosopher fellow who sat there.

'*Hrrrrm!* I'm taking Mother to the sea,' the little man told him.

'Why do you want to go there?'

'*Hrrrrm!* The sea is something very special,' the little man answered him. 'It is full of music and strange songs and stories, full of shadows and movement. My mother is very fond of it.'

'You love it too, don't you, little man?' said the philosopher.

'Well,' the little man replied, 'the more I hear my mother talk about it, the more the thought of it swells inside me, all glowing and wonderful.'

Then the philosopher shook his head. 'Go back, go back, little man,' he cried, 'because the wonderful things are always less wonderful than you hope they will be . . . The sea is less warm, the joke less funny, the taste is not as good as the smell.'

The old pirate mother called from the wheelbarrow, waving her cutlass.

'I must go,' the little man said shyly.

Off he ran, and as he trundled his mother away, he noticed that two buttons had popped off his coat.

Something new came into the wind scent.

'Ah, there's the salt!' His mother sniffed the wind. 'There's nothing as joyful as a salt sea wind.'

ly they came over a hill . . . Suddenly

nly stare. He hadn't

of the blue-

d roll like

each.

d

wave of it, the fume and the foam of it flooded into him and never left him again. At his feet the sea stroked the sand with soft little paws. Farther out the waves pounced and bounced like puppies. And out beyond again and again the great, graceful breakers moved like kings into court, trailing the sea like a peacock-patterned robe behind them.

Then, with joy, the little man and his mother

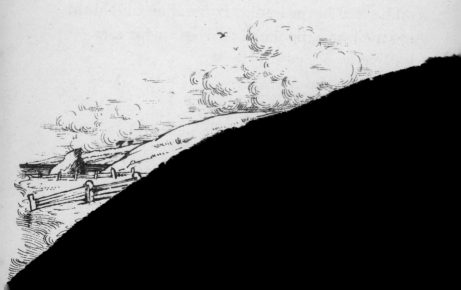

danced hornpipes along the beach. How the little man's neat clothes grew wild and happy to be free.

A rosy sea captain came along. 'Well, here are two likely people,' the captain said. 'Will you be my bo'sun, madam? And you, little man, can be the cabin boy.'

'*Hrrrrm*, thank you!' said the little man.

'Say "Aye, aye, sir!"' roared the captain.

'Aye, aye, sir!' smartly replied the little man as if he had never had a '*Hrrrrm!*' in his throat. And then he sang as he twirled on his toes.

'No wonder that
I dance on my toes.
Goodbye Mr Fat
And figures in rows,
Figures in rows
And ink's blue gleaming.
For where the sea goes
Is beyond all dreaming.'

So Sailor Sam went onto the ship with his pirate mother and the sea captain, and a year later somebody brought Mr Fat a letter that had been washed ashore in a bottle.

'Having a wonderful time,' it read. 'Why don't *you* run off to sea, too?'

And if you want any more moral to this story, you must go to sea and find it.

The Boy with
Two Shadows

There was a little boy who took great care of his
shadow. He was quite a careful little boy with
his buttons and shoes and all the odd pieces.
But most especially he was careful with his
shadow because he knew he had only one, and
it had to last him his life. He always tried to
manage things so that his shadow didn't trail in

the dust, and if he just couldn't keep it out of the dust he hurried to get to a clean place for it.

This boy took such care of his shadow that a witch noticed it. She stopped the boy on his way home from school.

'I've been watching you,' she said. 'I like the way you look after your shadow.'

'Well,' said the boy, trying to sound grown-up, 'the way I see it is this – it's the only one I've got. And it's going to have to last me a long time.'

'True! True!' said the witch, looking at him with great approval. 'You're the lad for me. The thing is, I want someone to look after *my* shadow while I am away on holiday. I don't want to drag that skinny old thing around with me. You know what a nuisance a shadow can be.'

'Mine isn't any trouble,' said the boy doubt-fully.

'That's as may be,' the witch declared. 'The thing is, I want to be rid of mine for two weeks, but I'm not going to leave it with just anybody – it's going to be left with *you*.'

The boy didn't like to argue with a witch.

'All right,' he said, 'but hurry back, won't you?'

The witch bared her teeth in a witch smile, which was quite wicked-looking, though she was trying to be pleasant.

'If you return my shadow in good condition,' she promised, 'you shall have a magic spell all of your own. I'll choose just the right one for you.' Then she fastened her shadow onto the boy's shadow, got on her broom, and made off, light and free as thistledown, with sunlight all around her and no bobbling black patch chasing at her heels.

The boy now had two shadows. One was his own. The other was the fierce, crooked, thorny shadow of the witch.

The boy had nothing but trouble with that witch's shadow. It was the worst behaved shadow in the world! Usually, it is a rule that shadows behave much as their people do – but the witch's wouldn't do that. When the little boy went to buy apples the witch's shadow rummaged among the shadows of the fruit. It put the shadows of all the oranges over beside the bananas, and mixed up the shadows of the peaches. Everything was all higgledy-piggledy.

The man in the fruit shop said, 'Throw that shadow out! How on earth am I going to sell oranges when they've got no shadows? And who's going to buy bananas with the shadows of oranges?'

The little boy didn't like to turn the witch's shadow loose on its own. He rushed out of the shop without his apples.

At home, all through tea, the witch's shadow stretched itself long and leaped all over the wall. It took the shadow from the clock, and the clock stopped. Then it terrified the parrot into fits, and pulled the shadow-tail of the dog's shadow.

'Really!' said the little boy's mother. 'I can't enjoy my tea with that ugly thing waltzing around the walls! You'll have to keep it outside.'

But the boy was determined to look after the witch's shadow. From then on, he had his tea in the kitchen on his own. He got so clever at

keeping the witch's shadow from getting into mischief and wickedness that at last it couldn't find anything wicked to do. Naturally this made it very cross.

Then suddenly, in spite of the little boy's care, the shadow thought of something new and mean – so mean that you would think even a witch's shadow would be ashamed. It started to pinch and tease and bite and haunt the little

boy's *own* shadow. It was terrible to see. The boy's shadow had always been treated kindly. His own shadow did not know what to do now about this new, fierce thing that tormented it, pushed it onto dusty places and trod on its heels as they hurried down the road.

One day the boy's shadow could bear this no longer. In broad daylight the boy, going home to lunch, saw his two shadows – short and squat – running beside him. He saw the witch's shadow nip his own smaller shadow with her long witch fingernails. His own shadow gave a great bound and broke away from his feet. Down the road it flew, like a great black beetle or a bit of waste paper flapping in the wind, then it was gone. The little boy ran after it, but it was nowhere to be seen. He stood still and listened to the warm summer afternoon. It was so quiet he could hear the witch shadow laughing – or rather, he heard the echo of laughing. (Because, as you know, an echo is the shadow of a sound, and sometimes the sound of a shadow.)

Well, you can just imagine. There was the little boy with only one shadow again – but it was the *wrong* shadow. His real shadow was quite gone, and now he had only the witch's left.

It was more like having a thorn bush at his heels than a proper shadow. There was nothing comfortable about this, and people stared and nudged one another.

As for the boy, he felt sad and lonely without his own shadow. He tried to like the witch's shadow, and he tried hard to take good care of it – but it was a thankless task. You might just as well try to pet a wild she-wolf or a thistle!

At last the witch came back. She wrote the boy a letter in grey ink on black paper, telling him to meet her that night at midnight and to be sure to bring her shadow with him. (Thank goodness it was a bright moonlit night or it might have been extremely difficult to find that wretched shadow, which hid away from him sometimes.) As it was, the witch whisked it back in half a minute less than no time. (In fact, it didn't even take her as long as that.)

'Now,' the witch said very craftily, 'here's

your spell.' She handed the boy a small striped pill, wrapped in a bat's wing.

'It's one I don't use much myself,' she said. 'But the boy who swallows that pill can turn himself into a camel. *Any* sort of camel, even a white racing camel – or a Bactrian or any sort of camel you like.'

The little boy couldn't help feeling it was a bit useless, in a way, to be able to turn himself into a camel. What he really wanted was just his own shadow back. He pointed out to the witch that her fierce shadow had driven his own gentle one away. The witch sniggered a bit in a witch-like, but very irritating, fashion.

'Well, my dear,' she said, 'you can't expect everything to be easy, you know. Anyhow, I feel I've paid you handsomely for your trouble. Run off home now.'

The boy *had* to do what he was told. He scuttled off sadly down the street to his home, carefully holding down the pocket where he had put the striped pill. It was bright moonlight and everything had its shadow – the trees trailed theirs out over the road, the fence posts pointed

theirs across the paddocks. The sleeping cows had sleeping shadows tucked in beside them. Only the little boy had no shadow. He felt very lonely.

At the gate to his house, he thought at first that his mother was waiting for him. A dim figure seemed to be watching out, peering up the road. But it wasn't tall enough to be his mother, and besides, when he looked again it wasn't there. Then something moved without any sound. He looked again. Softly and shyly as if it was ashamed of itself, his own shadow slid out from among the other shadows, and sidled toward him. It slipped along, toe-to-toe with him, just as it had always done.

The little boy thought for a moment:

He was free of the witch's shadow.

He had a magic trick that would turn him into any sort of camel he liked – if he ever wanted to.

And now he had his own shadow back again!

Everything had turned out for the best. He was so pleased he did a strange little dance in the moonlight, while, toe-to-toe, his shadow danced beside him.

Mrs Discombobulous

There was once a very cross woman called Mrs Discombobulous. Oh, she was a scold, a shrew, a vixen and a virago – and a proper tyrant and tartar to her poor husband (whose name was Mr Discombobulous). She niggled and naggled him day and night, from first yawn to last. He was ragged, poor-spirited, uncivil, unkempt and unkind, if you listened to what his wife said about him. Mrs Discombobulous's tongue, people said, was as sharp as a barber's razor, and three times as long. Mr Discombobulous used to sit

in silence, listening to her and staring out hard
from under his hat-brim while she scolded him,
and then he would stamp out and go and meet
his friends, who were all sorry for him, because
of Mrs Discombobulous and her scalding,
scolding ways.

Mr Discombobu-
lous would shake his
head and say to the
people next door,
'D'you know what she
said to me *today*?
Can you *imagine* what
she called me?' And all
his friends would
crowd around to listen
to the dreadful words
of Mrs Discombobu-
lous.

'Oh!' they gasped.

'Ah!' they breathed in mock amazement and
horror.

Well, one day Mr Discombobulous bought
his wife a washing machine, and of course she

had to try it out at once. So she put in some water and washing powder and clicked the switch. The machine started up . . . PRROOM! prroom! PRROOM! prroom, PRROOM, prroom! Inside the machine a swishy-swashy thing went 'Swish-swash, do the wash! Swish-swash, do the wash!'

This was all very right and proper, but suddenly the machine made a loud, grinding sound and went 'P-p-p-p-p-p-p-p-p-p-p-p-p' and started to throw soap bubbles and fountains of water in all directions.

'Well, Mr Tomfool Noodle!' snapped Mrs Discombobulous to her husband. 'Something is stuck. See what it is!'

'Yes, dear!' said the obliging Mr Discombobulous. Before he could get to the machine, he was swept aside by the thin brown right arm of his fierce and thistly wife.

'You'll only make things worse!' she yelled. 'Let *me* at it!' And she peered into her new washing machine and felt under the water.

There was Mrs Discombobulous, feeling round in the water, while Mr Discombobulous

stood patiently behind her. Then suddenly the machine started going 'PRROOM, prroom, PRROOM, prroom!' as before, while the swishy-swashy thing went 'Swish-swash, do the wash!' and lo and behold, before you could say 'Jack Snaprabbit!' Mrs Discombobulous was

63

PROOOMED and swish-swashed into the water.

Of course she shut her eyes. (This is the first thing you must do when you fall into a washing machine.) Then, as she was whirling around and around – this way and that way – in the machine, she thought – and thought *hard*. 'Halloo! Hallay! It's NOT, I say!'

She opened her eyes and saw to her wonderment that flames were jumping up all around her. So she jumped too. (This is the first thing you do when you find yourself in a fire instead of the washing machine you tumbled into.)

Where was Mrs Discombobulous *now*?

Under a dark sky, under strange stars, standing in a circle of gypsies. They were sitting around a campfire, and it was out of this campfire that she had just jumped. Cleverkangeroo-Mrs Discombobulous! Naturally the gypsies were amazed to see her, and she was just as amazed to see them – but she never showed it for an instant as she glared at them, and at their shadowy world that bounded off into the darkness all around her.

'Ho!' she said furiously. 'What are you all looking so glum about? It isn't raining. It isn't cold. I thought gypsies were *gay* people – not a miserable set of long-faced owls goggling around a campfire.' And she smoothed down her apron with her red, strong hands, and then folded her arms, so that her bony elbows stuck out like swords.

'Come on! What's the matter with you?' she snapped. 'Can't you speak? Or are you as big a set of lolling molly-mawks as you look?'

The chief gypsy got to his feet. He was strong as a bull, and as brown as a bear, but he was utterly dumbfounded by the sight of Mrs Discombobulous leaping, weasel-quick, out of his campfire. He spoke softly, and in a wheedling voice, because, like everybody else, he was already afraid of Mrs Discombobulous and her scouring glowering tongue.

'Yes, lady,' he said, 'here we all sit, very gloomy and sad; you see, we had among us a gypsy princess, Miranda. She was a wild flower, lady – a princess of wind and water – and we loved her.' He stopped to wipe away some tears.

'But she has been stolen from us,' he went on, 'by the Baron – the lord of the Castle, who plans to marry her next week. She herself wants to marry a young gypsy of our gypsy band and to live the wild, free life. Therefore it seems to us sad that she should be the Baron's wife and not a gypsy any more. A prisoner she may be now, but when she is his wife she will be a prisoner forever.'

Mrs Discombobulous looked crosser than before.

'You're a poor lot, you are,' she declared, 'moping here and doing nothing about it. A dismal, sullen sort of gypsy crew, not at all high-class, sitting all mumpish and dumpish around a campfire! I'd be off to this Baron if I were you and quickly put him to rights. I wouldn't stand it, *I* wouldn't. But you . . . *why* you might as well be a pack of earwigs, or poor dumb giraffes.'

'Lady, lady,' the gypsy chief cried, flinging up his hands in despair, 'the Baron isn't a listening sort of man, and his butler wouldn't even let us in to see him. What are a pack of raggle-taggle gypsies to the lord of the Castle?'

Mrs Discombobulous stood thinking, like a little sharp bristly thistle-woman, all flickery in the firelight.

'I'll tell you what!' she said. 'There isn't any

reason why I should bother about a pack of rascally ragamuffins like you – thieves as well, like as not, and probably not washed. (I can't bear dirt.) But I don't like the sound of this precious Baron. He sounds like a scoundrel, and spoiled to me, and as if he'd be the better for a setback. So if you'll take me to his house I'll speak to him. Oh yes, *I'll* speak to him!'

The gypsies saw at once that Mrs Discombobulous was just the person to speak to the Baron on the subject of their gypsy princess Miranda. He would not be able to shut his ears to the scratchety, ratchety voice of Mrs Discombobulous. So they led her to the castle door with its golden knocker and big golden bell. But Mrs Discombobulous disdained the knocker. 'Cheap, gimcrack thing!' she sniffed as she kicked at the door with her hard, pointed shoe.

An icy-faced butler answered the door. He turned up his nose at the ragged throng of gypsies, but he could not turn it up at Mrs Discombobulous. She could deal with a thousand such frosty fellows. Before she had

spoken more than a dozen words, that butler was scurrying up the great hall, faster than he had ever gone before. The portraits of the Baron's ancestors stared down in haughty

surprise at Mrs Discombobulous, but not even an ancestor could meet her snapping gaze without feeling uneasy.

The butler's eyes rolled nervously as he opened the dining room door. He looked like a man with a savage, biting dog at his heels – but about that he had no need to worry, for Mrs Discombobulous had never bitten anyone – yet.

The young Baron was at dinner, sitting at the head of a long table. At the foot of it sat the

gypsy princess Miranda, her dark head bent with sadness. She was a singing bird in a cage – a creature of air and shadow – shut up in a bright room and unable to be free again. The young Baron wore many bright rings and Miranda's brown hands were bare. Yet her fingers sparkled more than his, with the shining tears she let fall upon them.

Up leaped the Baron in dismay and anger, when Mrs Discombobulous marched in, and the gypsies crowded at the doorway.

'Who on earth are you?' he shouted.

'Are you the Baron – the lord of the Castle?' Mrs Discombobulous asked abruptly.

'Yes, I am!' he answered furiously, 'and I – ' but she interrupted him.

'Oh, I *thought* you were – I knew you were! You have just the spoiled, nasty look I would have expected, for all your fine clothes (and they aren't so very fine after all . . . tinsel and tawdry, I call 'em).

'However,' she went on firmly, 'I didn't come here to advise you about your style of dress, but to take this young woman home.'

Mrs Discombobulous shifted her position to a firm stance directly in front of the Baron, and glared down at him. 'Really,' she said, 'I can't think what the world's coming to when a poor girl – and a good one, too, as you can see by her face, the pretty dear – is carried off without so much as a please, or a by-your-leave, or even a thank you, by a giddy, humbug snip of a young lord who imagines himself a fine romantic fellow no doubt, but as anyone can see, he's an ass in a lion's skin, a wolf in sheep's clothing, and a snake in the grass . . . NOW SIR, will you let the lass go?'

'By thunder, I won't,' began the Baron. 'I won't and I shan't! And as for you, *you* can . . .'

'Won't! Shan't!' screamed Mrs Discombobulous as shrilly as a railway engine and much less musically. 'Do you forget, my lord, that *you* are supposed to be a gentleman? I say "supposed", because anyone can see at a glance that you are NOT one. I can read your face like a book, my lord, and believe you me, it's not a pretty story. It's a plain face to begin with, and your forehead shows you're a fool and a knave, your eyes tell me you're a scapegrace, a scallywag, a scamp – oh, and a bully too. Your big nose is that of a lawless, disorderly altogether discreditable IDIOT, and your weak mouth declares you are a shameful, felonious, reprehensible rascal. Moreover, you have the shoulders of a coward, and the legs of a camel, and you have a very slovenly, careless way of speaking.'

Mrs Discombobulous now rose to her full

height, and, placing a strong right hand on the Baron's shoulder, she said, in a low cozening voice, 'But if there is the least crumb of goodness in you (and I'm sure there isn't, but I'm willing to give you a chance to prove me wrong) you'll set this girl free – try to redeem yourself, in some small part, my lord, and maybe someone will yet think well of you – and even *like* you – though it's not what I'd call possible.'

'I'm not to be bullied – ' began the young Baron, but now he spoke in a feeble, peevish voice.

'Bullied?' yelled Mrs Discombobulous. 'And who's trying to *bully* you? D'you call being spoken to for your own good being BULLIED? Upon my word, my lord, you try me hard. I'm known as a reasonable woman, my lord. Large-hearted, admittedly; self-denying and high-minded, too. But above all else, reasonable! That's why I've kept my temper and not scolded you as yet, richly though you deserve it. But you are making my temper slip its moorings, and even a reasonable woman has her limits, my lord, and shortly I feel I shall be very sharp with you, if you don't stop your argie-bargie and let that gypsy girl go free.'

The thought that Mrs Discombobulous had not yet lost her temper, and the dread of what it would be like if she did, struck the young Baron almost dumb.

'You can go!' he said hoarsely to Miranda. She lifted a face still wet with tears, but happy now, like sunshine and summer seen through a mist of rain – and then she ran to the arms of her friends.

Off they went, light-foot down the hall. The young Baron would never catch her now, for she would fade into the forests and hedges with the other gypsy people, and marry her young man and travel far from his lands.

As she watched Miranda go, Mrs Discombobulous felt very strange – as if someone had seized her by the hair and by the seat of her skirt and was pulling like anything. She knew at once what it was, and shut her eyes on the Baron, giving a sarcastic laugh as she did so.

When she opened them again, Mr

Discombobulous was heaving her out of the washing machine.

'You fell into the water, my love,' he murmured.

'Oh!' said Mrs Discombobulous.

'Well!' said Mrs Discombobulous.

'I *know* I did, you fool!' said Mrs Discombobulous.

Then she was silent, and thought for a

moment. 'Am I a bad-tempered old woman?' she asked her husband, almost softly.

'There never *was* one with a more nasty temper than you,' he replied proudly.

A small smile flickered like winter sunshine over the face of Mrs Discombobulous. Then she said, 'Would you like me to change? It would be difficult, but I'm a strong-minded woman, Mr Discombobulous, and I could do it.'

It was the turn of Mr Discombobulous to think for a bit.

'It would be peaceful,' he said at last, 'I give you that . . . oh, so peaceful!'

And did Mrs Discombobulous change her fierce scalding ways and stop nagging and scolding her husband?

What do *you* think?

Hello, I'm Smudge

Would you like to hear about my book club?

It's for 4-8 year-olds and you get your own badge, membership book and a Club magazine four times a year.

It's packed with stories, puzzles and competitions.

You get a chance to buy new books!

And there's lots more! For further details and an application form send a stamped, addressed envelope to:

The Junior Puffin Club,
P.O. Box 21,
Cranleigh,
Surrey,
GU6 8UZ